ONE SHOT

TANYA LANDMAN

Barrington Stoke

First published in 2019 in Great Britain by
Barrington Stoke Ltd
18 Walker Street, Edinburgh, EH3 7LP

www.barringtonstoke.co.uk

A CIP catalogue record for this book is available
from the British Library upon request

ISBN: 978-1-78112-851-0

Printed in China by Leo

For Isaac and Jack

1.

By the time I came into this world, bawling and bloody, Ma was tired of raising babies. She'd had three in five years and one of them had died. I was the fourth. Ma's milk dried up when I was no more than a week old and after that I depended on the cow. Ma took sick and couldn't even rock me in my crib. So, first thing every morning, Pa filled a bottle, strapped me to his chest with Ma's shawl and took me along with him. I grew from baby to child out in the woods with Pa, listening to the birdsong and breathing in his smell along with the sweet scent of pine.

Pa was a quiet man. Say "quiet" to some folks and they think meek. Mild. Timid. Pa was none of those things. He didn't waste breath on words, but when he did speak, every last syllable was worth hearing. I never once saw him fidget or make a move that wasn't necessary. But

Pa's stillness was like that of a tiger. There was a powerful strength to it. I don't mean he was menacing; I mean he was mighty. Nothing seemed to scare him.

One time, when I was maybe four years old, Pa and I were out setting traps in the woods. The wind changed direction and a strong animal stink came drifting towards me. I wasn't far from Pa, not really. But then I heard the crunching of something heavy walking over dead leaves, and a bear came strolling through the undergrowth. That small distance between my father and me suddenly seemed like a hundred miles.

The bear stopped. Sniffed. Looked right at me. I felt a scream growing in my chest, but Pa breathed out slow, through his teeth. He said, as soft and calm as could be, "Come here, Maggie. Nice and slow." And he smiled like there was nothing at all to worry about.

I fixed my eyes on Pa's and he held me in his gaze. He pulled me in like a fish on a line, until I was by his side. The bear had come closer by then, but Pa wasn't inclined to rush. Slowly, he loaded his rifle. He poured a charge of powder into the barrel, dropped in a wad of cloth and a bullet and rammed it all down. Pa was talking to the bear the whole time. "I'm doing this just in case," he told it. "I don't want to go shooting you if I don't have to." Pa put a cap into the lock and pulled back the hammer so it was cocked and ready. But he didn't take aim. Instead, he sat himself down on the ground next to me, leaned against the tree, raised his face to the sun and yawned like he had no troubles in the world. The bear took a long, long look at him, then turned away.

"That's right," Pa said. "We ain't your next meal. And we ain't gonna hurt you none. You go your sweet way and we'll go ours."

The bear shuffled off into the trees and I breathed an almighty sigh of relief.

"I'm glad you didn't have to shoot it," I said.

"So am I," Pa replied with a laugh. "This old rifle will take out a pigeon or a squirrel well enough. I ain't sure it could bring down a full-grown bear. Heck, it would be more use as a club! I could have whacked that old bear to death."

2.

My father and I were still crying with laughter by the time we reached home. But before we went into the cabin Pa said, "Not a word to your mother." The thought of how she'd react to us meeting a bear wiped the smiles off both our faces.

Ma was the opposite of Pa. True, she was quiet. When we were in town, she didn't speak unless she was spoken to. She was modest. Ladylike. Yet in her quietness there was a kind of roaring rage.

The wooded rolling hills that surrounded our cabin were a place of wild wonder to me. As close to the Garden of Eden as I could imagine anywhere on earth. But Ma had been born and raised in a city on the east coast. She liked tall buildings, straight roads, stores and hotels and rows of houses with neat yards edged by picket fences. I never could figure out why she'd married Pa and moved into the wilderness. I guess she must have loved him, but sometimes it seemed that any soft feelings had been washed away in a flood of chores. All that was left in her was duty and the desperate desire to be respectable. Ma hated every inch of the county she found herself trapped in. I guess, deep down, she was afraid. At night, she'd flinch if an owl called or a fox barked. And my brother Alexander and my sister Katherine had sucked in her fear with her milk. They didn't like the big woods any more than she did. They eyed the trees sideways, as if there was something hiding behind them – something with teeth and claws and an empty belly desperate to be filled. Something that would leap out and swallow them whole. Any time they had to pull up a tree seedling from the patch Pa had ploughed, they did it like an act of revenge. If they had to help fell a tree for timber, they did that with such a grim joy it was like watching a public hanging.

I didn't understand my family and they didn't understand me. We didn't even look alike. They were blue eyed, pale skinned and had white blonde hair. Mine was the same russet brown as Pa's and I had a string of freckles across my nose in the exact pattern of his. When I looked into Pa's eyes, it was like looking in a mirror. I recall one time when we'd gone to the store and a stranger cracked a joke about how no one would ever question who my father was. We were as alike as two peas in a pod, that stranger said. I'd been christened Margaret Anne McGregor, but after that trip to the store, Pa took to calling me Little Pea.

3.

It was almost half a morning's drive to church, yet Ma insisted we leave paradise and make the journey there every Sunday. By dawn, Ma would have her three children dressed in clean clothing, our faces and necks scrubbed raw. Alexander's hair would be slicked smooth, mine and Katherine's plaited so tight that our eyebrows were pulled up into startled expressions. I feared my scalp might be ripped in two if I sneezed. Pa's collar was always starched so stiff he could barely turn his head.

In a creaking cart on a rough track, that journey was long and painfully hard on the buttocks. When we got there, the pews were no more forgiving. The sermons lasted for all eternity and were full of hellfire and damnation. The God our preacher talked about was not one of peace or love or merciful forgiveness for our sins. Jesus seemed to have been wiped from the pages of his Bible.

After we'd all been blistered by his words, we'd troop out of the church and then there would be the endless talk in the graveyard. Long adult conversations about things that didn't interest me. I had to stand and listen without fidgeting or fussing or making a sound.

But we didn't make it to church *every* Sunday. There were times when the cow had kicked the fence down overnight and it would need mending. Or maybe the horse had gone lame and Pa couldn't hitch him up to the cart. It was downright strange how often that cow timed her misdeeds and the horse his misfortunes for a Sunday. If we couldn't make the trip to church, Pa would go off and do whatever it was needed doing. Ma would have me, Alexander and Katherine kneeling and praying on the cabin floor for what felt like sun up to sun down.

But there was one Sunday when the hog ran off into the woods and Pa needed help fetching it back.

We were lined up on the porch, ready to go to church. The horse was hitched to the cart and

Pa was just climbing up on to it when there was a sudden grunting from the sty.

Pa yelled, "The hog's getting out!"

She was just nosing at the gate as he ran across the yard. Pa moved terrible slow. By the time he reached her, the hog was out of the pen.

"Hey, Pea!" Pa said. "Come help."

"It's the Lord's day," Ma screamed.

"Tell that to the hog," Pa said. "I ain't losing all that bacon."

He slipped in the mud, accidentally giving the hog a mighty whack on the rear. She squealed and broke into a run and the piglets were skittering along beside her.

Now I could see that Pa was being awful clumsy. Seemed to me he wasn't so much rounding the hog up as chasing her off.

But he'd called me, so I darted off the porch before Ma could grab me by my plaits and nail them to the wall. And then I was running, running with Pa and the hogs through the woods in my Sunday best. Running and laughing and bursting with excitement at the sudden and unexpected freedom. I had a stitch in my side by the time we reached a clearing.

Pa stopped running then. And the moment we stopped chasing her, the hog ground to a halt. She looked at the two of us as if we'd gone plum crazy. Then she started truffling in the undergrowth. The piglets chased each other in circles for a while, then lay around dozing in the spring sunshine.

Pa sat himself down.

"You do that on purpose?" I asked.

Pa gave me a guilty-looking smile. "Don't go telling your ma," he said. "I just couldn't stomach another morning of the preacher's sin and damnation. Not when the sun's shining and the spring is bursting out all over. Guess that makes me a sinner, don't it?"

"You and me both," I said.

"Guess I'm a little crazy too," Pa added. He ran his hand over the mossy log he was sitting on. "You know, when I built the cabin I apologised to the trees I cut down. I could almost hear them screaming every time the axe bit in to the bark. Guess that makes me a savage. The Indians used to talk of spirits. Everything living, breathing, in its own way, with its own soul – animals, birds, trees, plants, even the rocks. I can more easily believe in that than I can in a God who'd go to all the trouble of creating Man just so he can burn in hell."

We sat in that clearing until the sun started to sink and the chill came down and the hog got hungry and decided to head home for her supper. We followed her back, looking for all the world like we'd been chasing her for hours.

Ma was tight-lipped with fury, but I didn't care. I didn't have to please her. I had Pa, didn't I? It didn't matter what Ma thought if Pa was on my side. He was my god: all-wise, all-knowing, all-seeing, immortal. It never occurred to me he might not be around for ever.

4.

It was November. There was a crackle of ice in the air that threatened snow, but Pa was confident that he could stay ahead of the weather. I normally rode with him on the cart, but when he headed off to town that day he went alone.

I know a parent ain't supposed to have a favourite child, but I was clearly Pa's. I was almost eight years old and we were dirt poor. We didn't celebrate birthdays and we barely nodded at Christmas except to pray. Yet I knew – I just knew – he was going to fetch me back something special. So I didn't fume and fuss when Pa told me to stay at home. I waved him off, my heart bursting with a child's thrilling excitement at the thought of a surprise present.

Just lately, Pa had recalled a song his mother used to sing, and he'd been whistling it between his teeth. It was something about blue ribbons and bonny brown hair. The chorus ran, "Oh dear, what can the matter be?" I'd caught the tune from him like a winter cold, so I'd be humming along. I'd make up my own words when I couldn't recall the proper ones, sending Pa into laughs that rocked him from head to toe.

All that day Pa was gone, the tune was stuck in my head, running over and over. I was in a daze of happy anticipation to begin with and that irritated the hell out of my mother. Ma gave me chore after chore but I did them all with a smile on my face and a song on my lips, which annoyed the devil out of Alexander and Katherine. With Pa out of the house, there was no one standing between my siblings and me. I could feel the threat of violence hanging in the air, but they couldn't hurt me. Not yet. There wasn't so much as a whispered word or sly pinch. They knew as well as I did that all I'd have to do was tell Pa. But I could feel their resentment in every heartbeat.

Pa had left at the crack of dawn. He should have been home not long after noon. But midday came and went and there was no sign of him.

The proper words of the song he'd been whistling started to take on a kind of grim weight.

"What can the matter be? Johnny's so long at the fair ..."

When the light began to fade and there was still no sign of Pa, those words started to clang in my head like a funeral bell.

It had been dark an hour or more when the blizzard hit the cabin. It blew straight from the east, hard and fast. All of us knew without anyone saying a thing that it would have caught Pa on the road long before it reached us.

I recall the wind screaming around the walls. Ma was muttering prayers over and over for God to protect Pa. I sat still and I sat quiet – as if by doing that, as if by concentrating real hard, I could bring him home safe.

It must have been near midnight when we finally heard the soft slow thud of hooves and the creaking of the wheels.

"Alan!" Ma said, and flung the door open, calling Pa's name over and over. But her words were thrown back in her face by the wind and the snow. A great flurry of flakes came rushing in through the door, but Pa didn't. He was sitting

on the cart, frozen solid. He couldn't speak.
Couldn't move. Ma was screaming for us to come
help.

We tried lifting him but couldn't get him
down. He was all tangled up. It took a while
to realise that Pa must have lost the use of his
fingers when the blizzard hit. He'd wrapped
the horse's reins around his wrists because he
couldn't grip them. I tried to free him, but just
then the horse's knees buckled. The poor thing
died right there between the cart's shafts, pulling
the reins tighter than ever. Out in the wind and
the snow, my cold hands took an age to untie Pa.
I was shivering so hard I thought all the teeth in
my head would crack, but finally we carried our
father in, laid him by the fire and tried to warm
him.

We burned every last log Pa had cut and
stored for winter in the days and weeks that
followed. But the cold had gone too deep.
Seemed there was no way to drive it out of him.
Day after day, night after night, he'd suck in the
warm air of the cabin. But when each breath
came out, there was ice in it. When spring
finally arrived, Pa was still in the grip of winter.

I was there when he breathed his last. Pa's eyes fixed on mine. His mouth moved as if he wanted to tell me something. I leaned forward to hear it. But there was nothing. Just a rattling in his chest followed by a puff of air in my face, chill as the north wind.

That was it.

Pa was gone.

Ma was left with three children to feed and clothe and care for on her own. And she had a new baby on the way.

Pa was a mighty man, but that blizzard beat him.

It beat all of us.

5.

I didn't shed a single tear when Pa died.

The morning of the day we laid him in the ground, Ma took the bunch of blue ribbons he'd bought for my birthday, dropped them in the stove one by one and watched them burn.

Later on, in the graveyard when we threw the earth on his coffin, Ma started wailing, howling out her anger and sorrow. She was tearing at her clothes, her hair. Ma and Katherine cried a blizzard of tears between them. Alexander tried to stand tall. He was twelve years old now and considered the man of the family even though he couldn't shoot straight or plough a clean furrow. As the grave was filled, he was gulping and choking on his grief.

Yet not a single drop of water fell from my eyes.

Pa and I understood each other. Our souls were cut from the same cloth. I should have been heartbroken, Ma said. She told the preacher that I'd already forgotten him. "Oh, Maggie's fine. Children get over things, don't they? He's gone clean out her mind. You'd think she never even had a pa."

Ma was so very wrong.

Pa dying was too big a thing for tears. I knew deep in my soul that there would never be any getting over it. The world that had seemed so full of magic, of beauty, of wonder, had become a place of bewildering horror. Solid earth was like quicksand under my feet. I couldn't rely on anything, trust anything. Nothing felt real or solid. I was a scooped-out shell. Brittle. Fragile. But I was neither hollow nor empty. I was filled with a scream that whirled in my belly and twisted in my chest and whistled through my head. The noise took out every thought, every feeling, every word. Pa's death was a hole torn in my life. It would never close up, never heal, never go away.

In time, I learned to edge round that hole. In time, I learned to stop myself tumbling into it head first by treading real careful. Yet it was always there. There was never any changing the fact that Pa was gone.

I was eight years old, but I knew there wasn't any point to weeping or wailing. There was nothing to be said. The only thing I could do was endure. Survive. And for a long time it looked like I wouldn't be able to do that either.

6.

Ma couldn't manage alone.

Pa had built the cabin, cleared the land, fenced the field, made it fit for planting. It had been hard, hard work. All the years he'd been sweating and labouring, the forest had stood there – watching, biding its time, waiting for the moment it could take it back. One pregnant woman and three children couldn't fight the force of nature. In the spring, the woods reclaimed our land inch by inch. Saplings sprang up in the cornfield overnight, brambles sprawled across the pasture. First Ma sold the cow. The hog. Then the land. And the cabin.

She rented us a much smaller place nearer town. The baby was born not long after. A little girl, name of Carrie. As soon as Carrie was weaned, Ma handed her over to Katherine to mind. My mother got herself a job looking after other folks' children. It didn't pay well. There was never enough money in her purse to put enough food in our bellies.

One particular night there was nothing on the table and there was no prospect of there being anything the next day, or the one after that.

Ma was in despair. She'd sunk down so far that all she was doing was waiting for us to die.

If death had come in the dark – if it had come fast and been painless – I wouldn't have objected. But hunger tore at my insides. It made Alexander whimper and Katherine snivel the whole night through. Baby Carrie didn't have the strength to make a sound.

When dawn came, the rising sun found a crack in the cabin wall. A beam of light pierced the darkness. I could see hungry pinched faces, with eyes too big for their heads. There was Ma, curled up in a ball, working hard to stay in dreamland. As long as she was there, she didn't have to face the day ahead.

But that ray of light showed something else too. It glinted along the barrel of Pa's rifle. It was old-fashioned even back then. A worthless thing that hadn't been fired since Pa was alive. Hadn't been cleaned, neither. It had just lain there on the shelf, rusting.

It seemed to be calling to me, but maybe hunger was making my thoughts a little crazy. I remembered Pa, his eyes fixed on mine, trying to tell me something before he died. And suddenly I knew what it was he'd wanted to say.

When Pa used to take me out hunting, we'd walk along, my palm in his, joy radiating from his skin. It filled Pa's soul – the wonder and beauty of the trees, the way the sun shone through the leaves and dappled the forest floor, the sound of birdsong. He seemed to grow taller with each step. At that moment I realised that he hadn't taken me along just for the pleasure of my company. He'd carried his rifle in one hand, with the gunpowder horn strung around his neck. Each time he'd shot anything, he'd whispered to me as he loaded, aimed, pulled the trigger. He'd been showing me how to do it. Teaching me. And now I could feel his presence here in the cabin. Hear him whispering, "Go on, Pea. You can do it."

I crept across the earth floor, reached up and fetched down Pa's rifle before Ma could stir. I strung the horn around my neck with the pouch of bullets. I let myself out without a word to anyone and walked into the forest alone. When I came to a clearing, I decided to load the thing.

I was eight years old and small for my age. That gun was taller than me. Pa had made loading it look so simple. I found it tricky as hell. I had to stand on a log to pour the gunpowder into the barrel. After that, I took a wad of cloth and a bullet. Ramming them down was a real struggle. With trembling fingers, I put a cap into the lock and pulled back the hammer.

Pa's rifle was cocked and ready.

I stood still, hardly breathing, waiting for something – anything – to cross my path that I could shoot.

I don't know how long I was there. Maybe five minutes, maybe five hours. Time was acting strange. I seemed to have slipped from one world into another. I half-expected to turn my head and see Pa pushing through the undergrowth. It was so silent. The moss was thick on the trees, brilliant green in that golden morning light. The world looked fresh-made and new. Then a squirrel came jumping from one tree to another.

It stopped to take a breather on a branch above my head.

Slow, slow, slow, I raised the rifle. And I heard Pa's voice again, whispering in my ear, "Don't think about it. Point the barrel like it's your finger. Breathe out. Squeeze the trigger real soft."

It was a pity he hadn't spoken to me when I'd been loading the thing. I'd put in enough powder to kill an elephant. When I fired the rifle, the blast knocked me clean off my feet. I was thrown backwards on to the forest floor. But while I was lying there – dazed and wondering if my ears would ever hear the same again – the squirrel dropped dead at my feet. There wasn't a mark on it. I'd shot it clean through the head. The bullet had gone in one eye and passed out of the other.

"Well, would you look at that?" I said aloud. "Didn't I do good, Pa?"

7.

I was so pleased with myself, I walked back
whistling a song through my teeth just like
Pa always did. I hadn't imagined what effect
hearing me would have. Ma woke up with the
tune ringing in her ears and I guess she thought
that the last few months had been nothing but a
bad dream. Alan was back from hunting. She'd
best get up!

Ma appeared at the door of the cabin with a
face as white as a sheet but eyes that were full of
hope. Her mouth had formed a shape. She didn't
say it – the word died before she could give it
breath – but I knew my father's name was on her
lips.

Then she saw me.

Hope vanished. The truth slapped her around
the face so hard she was bent in two by it. And
Ma blamed me for that. A cold, bitter rage took

a hold in her heart. It made her vision skew sideways.

When Ma saw the squirrel in my hand, she didn't see food and she didn't see salvation. She saw a girl with a gun and it shocked her to the depths of her soul. Ma – like everyone else in the whole darned country – knew that a woman's place was in the home. A girl should be by her mother's side – cooking, cleaning, sewing, dreaming of her future husband and the children she'd raise. And yet there I was with a gun and a dead squirrel, having gone out alone into the wilderness just like I was a man. Ma had thought me cold before. Heartless. Unfeeling. Now she knew I was unnatural. A freak.

It was me that had to skin the thing, me that set the squirrel sizzling in a skillet over the fire. My mouth was watering, my belly was rumbling – that fresh meat smelled so good! I knew one squirrel between four people and a baby wouldn't be enough to fill any of our bellies, but it would take the edge off the hunger tearing at us. They ate it fast and I assumed they were grateful.

I picked up the rifle, meaning to go straight out again, but Alexander blocked the way. "You're not to go."

"What?" I said.

"She's shaming us, ain't she, Ma?"

I almost started laughing. I glanced at my mother, but she was looking at Alexander and nodding. Katherine was rocking baby Carrie and staring at me with accusing eyes and squirrel grease gleaming on her lips. "You're shaming us," Alexander said again.

"I ain't shaming you," I told him. "I'm saving you. We all got to eat, don't we?"

Katherine and Alexander looked at Ma. Her face was set.

It seemed Ma would rather starve respectably than live with shame.

I was mystified. The way I saw it, God had shone a sunbeam into the cabin to light up the rifle. He'd put Pa's voice in my head, telling me how to shoot the thing. God's hand had surely steered my bullet. If it was good enough for God, it was good enough for me. And where in the Bible did it say *Thou shalt not be unladylike?*

Of course, I didn't say all that. I was a child – I didn't have the power to persuade Ma round to my way of thinking. All I said was, "I'm helping, ain't I? Can't you just let me?"

Ma's eyes narrowed into slits. But her voice softened. "You want to help?" she asked.

"Yes, ma'am," I said, feeling suddenly hopeful. "I'll do anything you want me to."

"Get your things," Ma said. "Come with me."

8.

My "things" consisted of a wooden bird Pa had once whittled for me and the pouch I'd sewn to keep it in. I had the clothes on my back and that was it.

When Ma and I left the cabin, I thought she wanted to be alone with me for a moment. I thought she'd changed her mind about me and the rifle. Maybe she had some kind of plan?

But Ma set off in the direction of town, walking so fast I had to run to keep up with her. I had no breath left for asking questions.

She kept it up for an hour or more. We passed right through town and were almost out the other side when she stopped in front of a building.

It was the most terrifying place I'd ever seen.

Three storeys high, with bricks so red they looked like they'd been made from fresh blood.

Rusted iron railings surrounded the grounds like a cage.

But it wasn't just the look of the place that caught in my throat. A stink of misery was hanging over it, shimmering in the air like a heat haze.

Pushing the gate open, Ma walked right in, nodding at me to follow.

My mother walked back out less than five minutes later.

She walked back out alone.

9.

My mother had left me in the County Infirmary. It was a charitable institution to protect and care for people who couldn't take care of themselves. Every waif, every stray washed up there – every sick man, woman or child, every piece of flotsam and jetsam cast adrift on humanity's tide. There were children whose parents had died. Babies who'd been abandoned on the doorstep in the dead of night. There were old people whose bodies were so broken and beaten up by hard work they could hardly even hold a spoon. And there were grown folks who weren't right in the head – who dribbled and cursed and spat and wept and screamed and didn't know how to keep from soiling themselves. If I'd been older, I might have found some pity in my heart, but I was eight. They terrified me.

Looking back, I can see that the folks running the place meant well. The superintendent – Mr Rogers – and his wife treated everyone with respect. They were good people with kind hearts, doing the best they could with what they'd been given. But what they'd been given was precious little. As well as the piss and the shit and the vomit and the bad food, the whole building stank of despair. It was in the bricks and mortar, the walls, the floors – every stick of furniture was drenched with sorrow.

But I didn't cry. I'd been imprisoned for the crime of being unladylike. I was struck dumb with shock.

I was taken to a ward where thirty other children were crammed three or four to a bed. I was small for my age, so they'd put me in with the littlest and for that I was grateful. One look around and I could see faces that were yearning for love, for kindness, for a gentle word, a smile, a story. To them, I was almost a grown-up. Children need something to pin their hearts on and, from the moment I walked in, thirty of them were stuck on me.

Over the next weeks and months I became their mother, or the closest thing they had to it. It was truly pitiful. Babies of one, two, three years old, and the best thing they had was a young girl who was so wounded herself she didn't know which way was up.

I kept my head down and I did what I was told. I bobbed and I curtsied and I didn't speak unless I was spoken to. My eyes were always lowered and I did the work I was given – I dusted and swept and washed floors. In between the cleaning chores, I stitched and I sewed every waking hour. When I fell asleep, I did it in my dreams too. I figured that if I behaved like a lady for long enough Ma would fetch me home. She had to. Eventually. Didn't she?

10.

Time passed. But in the infirmary each hour
seemed to last a day. Each week stretched out
for a hundred years. I was working indoors, so
I couldn't see the passing of the seasons or feel
the changing of the weather. I couldn't hear the
birdsong.

I knew I was getting older and taller because
I outgrew my clothes. I had to make myself a
new dress and pinafore and then had to let the
hem down and the seams out. But I don't know
exactly how long I'd been there or how old I was
when a man walked into the place with his wife
on his arm.

She was a dainty little thing – with fine bones
and a sweet face – but her belly was so big she
looked ready to pop. The man said they were
looking for someone to help with the chores, and
it was obvious why.

Mr Rogers, the superintendent, called all the girls in the place together. We lined up and I kept as quiet as a mouse – my eyes down, my hands held in front of me, acting like a lady. I was strong but I was small. I didn't expect to be chosen. Ma had sent me away – why would anyone else want me? I had not a shred of hope in my heart.

The man and his wife went on down the line of girls. Passed me by. Got to the end of the room and spoke with their heads together, whispering. She nodded in my direction and her husband turned on his heel and came back alone. He stopped in front of me. Dropped down on his haunches so his face was level with mine.

He smelled of wood smoke. Of pine. Of fresh air and home-cooked food.

He smelled like Pa.

When I breathed him in, I was dizzied by a yearning so strong I had to shut my eyes.

"What's your name, child?" the man asked.

"Maggie, sir," I said.

"Can you read and write?"

Pa had been teaching me, but I hadn't got far. I'd forgotten almost everything since he'd died. "No, sir," I said.

"Want to learn?"

"Yes, sir."

At that point, Mr Rogers gave a small cough. The man stood and turned to him with his eyebrows raised in a question.

In a voice that was low – but not so low I couldn't hear every word – Mr Rogers said, "You won't want that one. She looks timid enough, but her ma said she's a wild thing. That's why she's in here – to stop her going off into the forest with her pa's rifle to shoot."

The man looked back at me. He smiled, and the sight was so unexpected my cold dead heart gave a little leap. "Can she aim straight?" he asked.

Mr Rogers sniffed. "Apparently so."

The man came back over. He hunkered down again so he could look me in the eyes. "We live in a small house in the big woods. Just me and Laura and the baby on the way. We could use another pair of hands. You work hard and we'll feed you and clothe you and give you an education. Does that sound fair?"

Oh my! I couldn't speak. My heart was hammering so hard I thought my ribs would break. I guess he thought I was hesitating, because he added under his breath, "If you want to hunt or shoot or set traps, I won't be making no objection." And then he smiled again and gave me a little wink.

I nodded. I still couldn't speak.

"That's agreed then," the man said. "I'll do what needs doing. Just as soon as it's arranged, you'll be coming on home with us."

Home.

That word was so fine I was close to fainting with just the sound of it.

I thought the man was Gabriel and Michael and all the archangels of heaven rolled into one. I thought he'd been sent by Pa to save me.

11.

I couldn't leave right away. Mr Rogers had to
write to Ma to get her permission. It was a full
two weeks before I could go. I counted every
single second in my head.

The morning finally came and the little ones
were crying and begging me to stay. But I was
so desperate to be out of there I could barely be
polite to anyone, let alone kind. Mr Rogers and
his wife walked me to the station, put me on the
train, told me how long the journey would take
and where I should get off. I had my pouch with
Pa's bird in it and a single dollar given to me by
Mrs Rogers so I could buy myself something to
eat on the way.

And then the conductor blew his whistle
and the train screamed in reply. We were off,
rattling along the tracks towards my new home.
I was so darned happy looking out of that window

at the countryside rolling by. It was springtime and the leaves were dazzling green like they were freshly sprung from the hand of God.

Around about noon, the train pulled in to a small town and a pie seller went on down the platform. I leaned out of the window, picked a big one and slipped the change from the dollar in my pouch. I'd never tasted anything so good as that pie.

And then, as the sun was starting to get low in the sky, we pulled in to the place I was supposed to get off at. I was a little anxious for a moment – what if he didn't come and get me? What if this was one big old joke?

But no – there he was, with his horse and cart and a big welcoming smile on his handsome face. It seemed to me that I could hear a heavenly choir singing. Climbing up onto the cart next to him was like being out with Pa. We drove along a track with the sun sinking lower between the trees and it was real pretty. I recall thinking that if I dropped dead at that moment I'd die happy.

And then we arrived at the house and his wife came out to meet us. She held a tiny baby in her arms that was bawling and red-faced and covered in sour milky sick. She handed the baby to me the moment my feet hit the ground.

I thought I was arriving in paradise.

It took less than two minutes for me to discover that Ma's preacher had got it wrong with his talk of fire and damnation after death. Hell was alive on earth, right here right now. I'd been dropped into the heart of it. And there was no salvation.

12.

I read someplace that sharks can smell blood in the water from a hundred miles away. I figure it's the same with people. If someone's brought down by sorrow, a human predator can sniff them out. I'd lost Pa. Ma had abandoned me. I couldn't have been any lower. When that married couple saw me standing in line in the infirmary, they scented blood. They could do whatever they wanted and I wouldn't put up any kind of fight. They knew I was already beat.

I don't like to think too much about that time. It's a strange thing. No matter how sinful those folks were, there's still some part of me deep down inside that burns with shame every time I recall them. It doesn't matter now how much I tell myself that they were bad people, rotten to the core of their souls, that they had no right to do what they did to an innocent child. I guess when you're as rock-bottom low as I was back then, you think you deserve the treatment you get. You believe you ain't worth more than the shit on the sole of the boot of the person who's kicking you.

Every morning, long before dawn, I got up, made the breakfast, milked the cows, washed the dishes. I skimmed the milk, fed the calves and the hogs, pumped water for the lot of them, fed the chickens, weeded the garden, fixed their meals. There was never any end to the work. Worst of all was minding that damned baby. It cried every waking moment. And when it slept it grizzled and whined. Looking back, I figure that child needed a little rocking and a little loving from its ma. But she was not the rocking or the loving kind. She'd feed it, her face wrinkled up with distaste, then hand it straight to me.

"Get it to sleep," she'd say.

And I was small, and the baby was heavy and awkward in my arms. It would spew its ma's milk down my back and then start bawling. And she'd plain refuse to feed it again until the required interval between meals had passed, saying it would get spoiled and she wasn't going to give in to its tantrums. She said it was my duty to keep it quiet. But that baby was hungry. And feeding it was the one thing I simply wasn't capable of. My failure got me beating after beating after beating.

13.

During the day, mostly it was just me and the wife and the baby. The husband would be in town, doing lord alone knows what.

But one time he came home early and caught her hitting me. He took me aside, said he was sorry. He'd find a way of making it better, and I believed him, darned fool that I was.

He took me out in the woods the next day. Said we'd go hunting. He shot a squirrel from point-blank range, blasting its head clean off.

"That's fixed supper," he said with a smile. "Guess now we can have ourselves a bit of leisure time."

Leisure time? What in the name of God was that? The idea of time being spare to sit around in was unfamiliar. I always had too much to do and too little time to do it in. A great weight of undone chores always bore down on me. Even now I could feel the washing that needed doing, the floor that needed sweeping, the weeds that needed pulling, the food that needed cooking.

But the man beckoned to me, saying, "Come on over here. Sit beside me. Fine day, ain't it? Feel the sun on your face. Listen to the birds."

He patted the log he'd sat himself down on and I did as I was told. He leaned towards me. The hairs on his arm brushed against mine.

"She ain't kind to you, is she?" he said softly.

How was I to reply? She was his wife. What could I say? Was this some kind of trap? I didn't answer. Kept my eyes on the ground. Watched a beetle crawl over the dead leaves at my feet.

"I thought the baby would soften her up," he said. "But motherhood has made her mean. I could use some kindness. Guess you could too. Tell you what. You be kind to me and I'll be kind to you. That sound like a plan?"

There was some meaning behind his words that I couldn't catch. But I nodded anyway. I even tried to smile.

And the next thing I knew he was holding me down and pushing up my skirt. And I was too small and too scared and too goddamned shocked to fight back. I shut my eyes. All I could see was snow on my lids. A blizzard was filling my head. And all I could think was:

He ain't being kind.

He ain't being kind at all.

14.

Spring passed and then the summer. Fall came and went and soon winter was on us, suffocating the house under a thick blanket of snow. I never once set foot off the place apart from the times the shark man took me out into the woods. The miserable baby grew into a miserable child that hung off my skirt while I worked, and oh lord did I work! I didn't have the time for a single thought in my head. At night, I was so dog-tired I didn't dream. I didn't even have the strength to wish to die or to pray to God to strike the two of them down.

One day when the snow outside had started to thaw, their miserable child stopped whining and screaming and fell as silent as the grave. A fever had taken hold and there was nothing I could do to ease it, no matter how hard the shark woman brought the poker down across my back. When the child started turning purple, she wrapped it in a blanket, her husband hitched up the horse and they both drove into town to find a doctor.

I was left alone.

Alone!

For the first time in almost a year there was no one here but me.

I had one shot at freedom.

I grabbed my pouch with the bird that Pa had made and the change from the dollar Mrs Rogers had given me and I ran.

The station was in town. I guess it would have made sense to head there and get myself on a train that would take me as far away as fast as possible. But I couldn't risk running into the pair of sharks I was escaping from. When I fled, I fled the opposite way, keeping to the places where the snow had melted. I didn't want to leave any tracks as I ran deep into the endless woods.

I had no idea where I was heading. The trees were so thick and the day so cloudy I couldn't see the sun. My only thought was to get away. I prayed, but not to God. I'd lost a little faith in him this last year. Instead, I prayed to Pa to watch over me, guide my feet, see me through the trees safe. Or if I met a bear and got myself killed, to make it be over quick so Pa could meet me in heaven.

I ran until I didn't have any more breath left in me. Then I walked, setting one foot in front of the other.

I kept going. And going. The days were still short and soon the light began to fade and the chill started to bite deeper. It got darker and darker, but I kept walking. Now I was falling over tree roots and banging my head on branches and could hardly see the hand I'd put out to protect my face.

Even then I kept going. Slower now. Much slower. Feeling my way forward.

And then at last I came to a place where there was a gap in the trees. I could hear it rather than see it at first. The air was different and the sound of my breathing wasn't muffled by bark and branches. And then one foot crunched on loose stones and the other foot hit something hard. I stopped, trying to make sense of it. And at that moment Pa must have let out a sigh because a hole cleared in the clouds and the moon shone down.

I'd reached the rail track.

Well, seeing this, I figured the town lay more or less to my left. So I followed the tracks right. Walking along here was easier than walking through the woods, but I was hellishly tired by then. I tucked my hands into my armpits because I couldn't feel my fingers any more. I didn't dare lie down and sleep. My breath was billowing out in clouds and it made me think of Pa's last icy gasp. If I stopped, I knew the cold would kill me like it had him. And it wouldn't be fast and it wouldn't be painless.

The moon came and went, and after a very long while the sky started to lighten. By the time the sun rose over the horizon, there was a town and a station in the distance.

15.

Forty-eight cents.

Forty-eight cents wasn't enough to get me home.

Forty-eight cents wasn't enough to get me anywhere.

If I'd cried – if I'd looked even a little ladylike – maybe the man in the station ticket office would have taken pity on me. But I'd been walking all night. My toes were poking out of the end of my boots and the nails were ragged and bleeding. I was scratched and filthy from running through the forest. I looked like a beggar and the man treated me like one. (Though why should someone down on their luck be less deserving of pity than someone who's slept all night in a comfortable bed? It is and always has been beyond me.)

I didn't know what to do or what to say. I didn't know where to go or what might happen next. I was beat. I just stood there, frozen, until the ticket seller flapped a hand at me like he was shooing away a fly.

I spun around and walked straight into the man standing in the queue behind me. My face hit his soft belly and he let out an "oof!" sound and put his hands on my shoulders to stop himself falling. The feel of a man's hands on my skin made me curl into a spitting, hissing mess of fear and rage.

But the man apologised to me.

He apologised to *me*.

I was expecting a slap or something worse. He was carrying a stick and my back was still smarting from the poker. But he took a step away and said, "I'm awful sorry, miss. I didn't mean to go getting in your way." His voice was so gentle and kind it sounded as sweet as birdsong.

I looked at him, slack-jawed with amazement. I must have resembled one of the crazy people from the infirmary.

"Did I hear right?" the man asked. "Do you not have enough money for your fare? Would you permit me to pay for your ticket?"

I still couldn't speak. I just stared.

"I don't mean to intrude," he carried on. "But I can see there's a problem here. I'd like to help you if I may."

I managed one word: "Why?"

He smiled. And it was a pleasant, open, honest smile. There was pity in it. And concern. "I've got a daughter of my own," the man said. "If she was in trouble, I'd like to think a kindly stranger would help her find her way home."

My mind was turning somersaults. I'd been taken in by a couple of sharks. What if he was another one, circling in the water, waiting for a chance to take his bite?

And yet what choice did I have? I could turn him down. But then what? Sleep on the streets? Walk back to Ma? The chances of me getting home alive and unharmed were zero.

No ... I was just going to have to believe that there were decent men in the world besides Pa, and that the man standing in front of me was one of them.

And if he wasn't? I laughed out loud. What could he do to me that hadn't already been done? I'd seen the worst of people. Yet here I was, still standing.

I took a chance. I trusted him. And that man truly was Gabriel and Michael and all the archangels rolled into one.

He asked where I was going and I gave him the name of the town closest to Ma. He bought my ticket. And then he rode in the train beside me, not saying anything – not intruding, not demanding attention or gratitude. He just watched out for me while I dozed in the seat next to him. He bought me a pie and it was the first thing in months I'd eaten that I hadn't prepared and cooked. It tasted so good and I gobbled it down so fast he bought me another.

When we finally pulled up at my station, he wished me well and said he hoped I'd get home safe. I envied that daughter of his. As I watched the train pull away, a fanciful thought drifted into my head: maybe I should have begged him to adopt me. But I hadn't even asked his name.

16.

When I knocked on the door of Ma's cabin, it was opened by a stranger. The woman inside told me my mother had moved house. She gave me directions to the new place. And when I got there I found out that my mother had married a man by the name of Mr Jeremiah Crawley.

Ma didn't seem to have much luck when it came to picking husbands. Mr Crawley had borrowed money from the bank and bought a small farm on the edge of the woods. He and Ma had settled down to raising children of their own. But he'd gotten sick not long after their wedding, so instead of being a blessing he became a burden. He couldn't save Ma from poverty or support the family. Instead, she just had one more mouth to feed, one more body to care for, one more baby on the way.

She was struggling to hold things together. Alexander was bigger and stronger than he'd been the last time I'd seen him, but he just didn't have Pa's skills or sense. He still couldn't shoot straight or plough a clean furrow. Katherine was doing the best she could to help Ma, but they were all stick-thin and miserable and I was the very last thing any of them wanted to see. I hadn't been home five minutes before I realised the only place I'd be welcome was the County Infirmary.

17.

Mr and Mrs Rogers were disappointed in me. When I arrived at the infirmary, they said they'd found me a good place with kind people and I'd gone off without a word! How could I? What was I thinking?

I stood there in the infirmary's office, hanging my head. They told me they'd expected more and how badly I'd let them down. I couldn't tell them what the shark man and his shark wife had done – I was too ashamed.

"Why'd you run away like that?" Mrs Rogers asked. "Were you homesick? Did you miss the other children?"

It was easier to have her believe a lie than try to tell even a fraction of the truth, so I nodded.

"Come along," Mrs Rogers said, and this time her voice was gentler. "Let's get you cleaned up before you see the others. You look like you've been dragged through a hedge backwards."

She fetched me clean clothes. She drew a bath and told me to get in it. As I undressed, she was talking, telling me the scrapes the little ones had gotten into while I'd been gone.

I wanted to get in that water, but my dress was stuck to my back and I couldn't get it over my head. Thinking I was clumsy with tiredness, Mrs Rogers came to help. She gave it a hard tug and the cloth ripped off my skin, pulling away the dried blood from that last beating.

I couldn't see how it looked, but it must have been bad because Mrs Rogers cried out in shock.

"Dear God!"

There was a moment's silence. She looked at me and I looked at her and there was no need for us to say anything. Suddenly her arms were around me and she was weeping into my hair and muttering over and over, "Oh, you poor child!"

And anyone else might have cried along with Mrs Rogers, but I guess I truly was unnatural and unfeeling, because I didn't. I couldn't. There was nothing in me but fury that I had to take love and comfort from strangers because my own ma couldn't give me none.

18.

Mrs Rogers took special care of me after that.
She treated me less like an inmate and more
like a valued member of the infirmary staff. She
gave me the schooling that the shark man had
promised, so I finally learned to read and write.
In return, I worked real hard: washing infirmary
windows, scrubbing infirmary floors, helping
with endless mountains of infirmary laundry.
It was a never-ending cycle of washing and
cooking and cleaning. I acted as meek and mild
and ladylike as it was possible for any female
to be. I sewed clothes for the little ones. I told
them stories and I tucked them into their beds
at night with a kiss on the forehead. I was never
still. Never idle. I never sat down unless I had a
piece of work in my hand – stitching a split hem,
darning a stocking, sewing on a button. Mrs
Rogers sometimes told me to take a break, have

a rest, but I didn't want time to think. If I worked myself to exhaustion, I didn't dream of the shark man and his shark wife and their goddamned baby. I didn't dream of anything at all.

Now, I didn't pay any heed to birthdays, so it was something of a surprise when Mr Rogers called me into his office one fine morning and told me that as I was sixteen years old I was a grown woman who could rightly stand on her own two feet. And, seeing as the infirmary was only there for folks who couldn't take care of themselves, it meant I had to leave.

For a moment, the thought of going out alone into the world terrified the life out of me. But then Mrs Rogers said I was welcome to stay on. I'd proved my worth over and over again these last few years. And if I stayed, she said I'd be paid like every other maid.

"Of course you might want to return to your mother," Mrs Rogers said. "And maybe you'll be thinking of getting married yourself some day soon, starting your own family. You'd be a wonderful homemaker. You don't need to decide now. Take some time to think it over."

Think it over? I hadn't thought anything over in years. I didn't know where to begin.

I'd lived as long in the infirmary as I had with Ma. And yet, if I stayed, I'd be one maid among so many. Life would stretch out in front of me, each day exactly like every other. Mrs Rogers had been kind. I had no doubt she truly cared about me. But when it came down to it, this wasn't home and Mrs Rogers wasn't family.

So where in the world did I belong?

When I went to bed that night, my head was spinning. I didn't think I'd sleep at all, but I fell into a slumber almost as soon as my head hit the pillow.

And I dreamed.

I was a child – maybe two, three years old – out in the woods with Pa. The light was coming through the trees and we were sitting on a mossy log. The morning air was cold and we didn't want our warm breath to make billowing clouds, so we were both holding it in. My chest ached with the effort. But Pa had told me that if we kept still for long enough, we might see the

fairies. And I could feel them all around me. I
could hear the rustle of their wings, the softness
of their gossamer clothes, as smooth as silk. I
could hear fairies muffling their laughter. I knew
that if I turned my head fast, I'd be able to see
them. But if I moved, I'd scare them away. So
I stayed next to Pa, perfectly still, feeling the
magic of the place flow through my veins.

When I woke up, I knew that Pa had put that
dream in my head. It was his way of telling me
to leave the infirmary. The trees were calling
me.

The place I belonged was out in the woods.

19.

The dream put me in an optimistic frame of mind. I told myself as I walked home that things would be different between me and Ma now I was a grown woman. She'd be glad of my help. Mrs Rogers said I'd be a good homemaker. Heck! Ma might even be proud of me. And absence makes the heart grow fonder, doesn't it? She'd surely be pleased to see me after all this time?

My happy thoughts lasted until I knocked on the door of the cabin. When Ma opened it, I saw that her feelings towards me hadn't changed. She might even have slammed the door in my face if her husband hadn't looked up and seen me.

Last time I was there, Mr Crawley had been too sick to get off the bed. He hadn't spoken a single word to me. But this time he was sitting at the table. He still looked far from well, but the smile on his face was welcoming.

"Maggie, ain't it?" Mr Crawley said. "Come right on in. It's a pleasure to see you."

Ma had been about to put supper on the table and Mr Crawley insisted that the family all budge up to make room for me.

I knew from gossip in the town that Alexander had left home a year or two back. He'd gone to the city to find work, but Ma hadn't heard from him in a while. Katherine had got herself married to a man who worked on the railroad.

I sat myself down opposite Carrie – the baby that Ma had been carrying when Pa died. Carrie was now almost the same age as I'd been when Pa had passed. She'd never known anyone but Mr Crawley as a father, but she was the dead spit of Pa. It felt odd looking at such painfully familiar features on the face of a stranger.

Besides Carrie there were three more children of assorted sizes who took Mr Crawley's looks. And a new baby who had Ma's white blonde hair and pale skin.

I was truly grateful for the noise they were making because that meal was about the most awkward I'd ever had.

The first thing Ma said was that if I was going to live with them – and she emphasised the "if" – I needed to pay my way.

Well, I'd expected to do that. I couldn't blame Ma for wanting me to pull my weight. Jeremiah Crawley seemed a good, kind man, but he was a sick one. I could see from the state of the place that things were real hard. I suspected that if they didn't improve sometime very soon they'd be in danger of losing the farm. I'd have gladly worked my fingers to the bone for them all if only Ma had smiled.

She put a pan of stew on the table and we sat there looking at it before digging in. It was grey and it didn't smell too good. There was some sort of bird in there, but it was hard to tell what kind. It had sure been left hanging for too long and was right on the edge of turning bad.

I looked at my stepfather, Mr Crawley, and asked, "You shoot that?"

"No," he said with a pained smile. He held his hands out so I could see how much they shook. "I never was much of a shot and I ain't up to hitting anything now. Your mother bought that from the store in town."

Ma cleared her throat. It seemed that shooting was still a sensitive subject. "I heard the Stewarts in the big house on the hill are looking for a girl," Ma said. "You can sew, can't you? Mrs Rogers wrote me and said your work was real neat. You know how to cook and clean – she taught you all that?"

"I know how to work," I replied.

I was so used to keeping things inside, acting like a lady. But an anger had started to grow in me and it might well have erupted. I could have said a whole lot of things I'd have regretted and we might even have fought. But there was no chance for that, because Mr Crawley cried out in sudden pain and put his hand to his jaw.

I thought maybe he'd bitten his tongue, but it was worse than that. He'd chewed down on a piece of meat and the darned bird was so full of buckshot he'd cracked his tooth on a lump of lead.

If that wasn't a sign from God, I was a corncrake.

"I'll go see the Stewarts first thing tomorrow," I promised.

I was lying.

I'd had my fill of skivvying for other folks. Oh, there was nothing wrong with cooking and cleaning, but anybody could do that. Yet I was the only one in the family who could put fresh meat on that table! I was a grown woman; I could make my own decisions. It didn't make any kind of sense not to use the talent God had given me. If I still had it, of course. I had a moment of doubt, but then I figured Pa had put that dream in my head. The woods had called me home. It was for a reason, wasn't it?

I'd find out in the morning.

20.

I walked softly and Pa was there with me every inch of the way. I could feel him smiling, nodding, encouraging me to go on. The woods were holding their breath and the little girl deep inside me still thought there were fairies just out of sight. But I was listening for prey now.

Jeremiah Crawley might have been a poor shot but he'd kept Pa's gun clean and oiled. For that I was truly grateful.

If I'd had any worries that I'd lost my skill, they vanished the moment I'd taken Pa's rifle off the shelf. It felt so natural to have it in my hand I almost wept with relief. That ease I'd had with the weapon when I made my first shot all those years ago was still with me.

That morning I killed two squirrels, one rabbit and four pigeons. I hit each one through the eye, one bullet apiece. Clean shots. Not a single crumb of buckshot peppering the flesh.

But I didn't take them home for the table. I wasn't ready to face that battle yet. Instead, I walked all the way into town. The sun was high by the time I stopped outside the Wagners' general store. Taking a real deep breath, I went on in.

They knew me well enough. I'd run plenty of errands around town for Mrs Rogers over the last few years, so Mr Wagner greeted me by name from behind the counter. Then he saw what I was carrying and his brow creased into a puzzled frown. He said, "What can I do for you today, Miss Maggie?"

An image of Ma filled my mind. She wasn't going to like this one bit. Hell, I might just be digging my own grave!

I stared at the floor. Mr Wagner's gaze felt as heavy as a lead weight pressing down on my head. And there were other customers coming in now, lining up behind me. It was too late to back out: I'd been seen, and gossip would already be sticking to me like tar. I could hear murmuring. Muttering. Folks weren't sure how to react to the sight of a sixteen-year-old girl with a gun. Were they going to laugh? Shout? Run me out of the place thinking I was a disgrace to my family?

But then Pa's voice was there in my ear: "Hold still. Keep calm. Breathe, Little Pea."

It didn't matter what everyone else thought if Pa was on my side.

But I wasn't sure how a respectable lady went about selling her kill to a storekeeper. I kept my eyes lowered, feeling the colour rise in my cheeks as I laid down my gun and put the pigeons on the counter one at a time. I set the squirrels each side and stretched the rabbit over top.

"What'll you give me for these?" My voice came out in a whisper.

There was a long silence while Mr Wagner stared at me. Eventually he said, "I heard you've moved back in with your ma. Did Mr Crawley shoot these?"

"No, sir," I said.

"Didn't think so. Then who did?"

"Me, sir."

Another long silence. I could feel Mr Wagner's eyes travelling up and down, taking in the leaves and brambles in my hair, my feet and legs spattered with mud.

"The bird you sold my ma yesterday was full of lead," I said. "Mr Crawley cracked a tooth. I shot all these clean, sir. Take a look."

There was a ripple of interest from the folks behind me when I said that. A woman piped up, "I had that same problem with the rabbit I bought last week." A man somewhere grunted in sympathy.

"If that one there is shot clean, I'll take it," the woman carried on. "I'd gladly pay more for something that I didn't risk losing a tooth over."

I could have kissed her for that. Turning round, I threw her a smile. I knew every face in town but not hers. I figure that woman was an angel sent by Pa.

Mr Wagner burst into a great belly laugh and roared, "Well, I'll be jiggered! Who'd have thought a little lady like you would be such a fine shot? Now I've seen everything."

"Will you buy them, sir?" I asked.

"Oh, I surely will." Mr Wagner opened his till and started dropping coins into my hand. He told me if I went out shooting again, he'd happily take whatever I could provide. And then he added quietly, "Folks like a bit of novelty. I think you just might be the next big thing."

21.

I knew I'd have to tell Ma what I'd been up to.
Otherwise, she'd find out soon enough. She didn't
get into town very often, but some helpful soul
passing the farm would be sure to tell her. So I
tried finding the right words as I walked back.

I knew gossip travelled fast, but on this
occasion it ran ahead of me like wildfire. By the
time I reached the cabin, I could hear a voice
coming from the open door. It was so loud with
outrage it carried halfway across the yard.

Taking a detour around the back so they
wouldn't see me, I heard Ma's nearest neighbour
declaring that I'd been seen walking into town
as bold as brass with a rifle under my arm and
almost more game than I could carry.

"You look surprised, Liza," the neighbour
screeched. "Didn't you *know*? Why, I assumed
you'd sent her! You mean to say ...?"

I was ready to run for the hills, but the neighbour was cut off by Mr Crawley. "I told Maggie she could go."

There was a silence. My stepfather's barefaced lie stopped me in my tracks. My mouth dropped open. I imagine Ma was just about scraping her jaw off the floor.

"You gave her *permission?*" the neighbour said.

"I did." Mr Crawley gave a dry wheeze that passed for a laugh in a man so sick. "You think a respectable girl like Maggie would go off without my say-so? We talked about it last night. She's a fine shot. God truly does work in mysterious ways. He's blessed Maggie with a talent. It would be an insult to the Almighty if she didn't use it."

I waited in the outhouse until the neighbour took her leave. It wasn't long: all the wind had been knocked from her sails by Mr Crawley. When the sound of departing cart wheels faded into the distance, I took my courage in both hands and went in to face Ma.

She was red-faced. Tight-lipped. She had her arms folded, her fingers pressing hard into her flesh.

All I wanted was for Ma to hold out her hands, embrace me, smooth my hair, tell me she was proud. I'd given up expecting her to love me, but a little liking would have gone one heck of a long way.

But she wasn't going to do that any time soon.

I don't know what we'd have done if it had just been the two of us. Maybe we'd have had ourselves a cat-fight. Maybe I'd have been thrown out. Or maybe I'd have decided to take off on my own.

What saved me and Ma from ourselves was Mr Crawley.

I figured Ma was madder with him than with me. She'd known for years that I was a freak. But her husband, taking my side? That was a new betrayal, one she hadn't expected, one she wasn't going to forgive.

Mr Crawley was worn out with sickness even before the neighbour's visit. Now he was dog-tired, his skin pale and yellow, his face looking waxy and wet.

"I'm not going to argue with you, Liza," he said. "We have children. Lord forgive me for not being able to provide for them the way I want to. I'm willing to let Maggie do anything she can to help keep a roof over their head."

My mother began to protest, "The shame of it!"

Mr Crawley held up his hand and Ma bit back the rest of her sentence. He said, "Maggie ain't selling herself. Shooting and whoring are not one and the same thing. Be reasonable, sugar."

Ma cared about how things looked. She minded about not only doing but being seen to do the right thing. And the right thing in her mind was to obey her husband. As long as Mr Crawley was alive, he was the head of the household and his word was law. I remember thinking that God must have a mighty strange sense of humour. The very desire for respectability that had broken Ma and me apart all those years ago had now saved me.

I went to bed that day with a smile on my face. I knew that as long as Mr Crawley was alive, I could carry on doing what I did best.

22.

Trouble was, Mr Crawley wasn't going to live that long. Ma was a good nurse. Pa had been at death's door when we brought him in from the blizzard and yet she'd managed to keep him alive all winter. I knew she'd keep her second husband lingering on for as long as possible. But I'd seen his wet, waxy look before. When people at the infirmary took on that sheen, their days were numbered.

Mr Crawley coughed most of that night and I lay awake wondering what I'd do with myself when he was no longer there to stand between me and Ma.

When the dark began to fade, I took myself off into the woods. I decided I'd cross that bridge when I came to it. For now, I'd push every thought out of my head apart from hunting and shooting.

So life went on.

I figured that town was a more dangerous place than the woods and that words could shred me worse than a bear's claws. So I minded how I behaved. I was modest. Polite. Shy. I dressed the same as when I'd been at the infirmary: like a girl, not a grown woman, wearing my skirts just down below the knee. It was partly practical: I couldn't go climbing over fallen trees or pushing through brambles in a corset and full-length dress. But I also thought it would do no harm if people thought me younger than I was. Folk were more forgiving to a child who did things that were out of the ordinary.

My plan worked, mostly. Word soon got round town and customers came into the store asking for game that had been shot by me. Of course, I wasn't popular with the blacksmith who earned a few cents on the side by pulling cracked teeth from folks' heads. And the other hunters looked at me sideways, but they wouldn't pick a fight with a girl.

Most people treated me like I was a novelty: a strange and curious thing, but nothing that threatened them. Some, like Mr Wagner, actively encouraged me. But there were also one or two ladies who'd cross the road if they saw me coming. Seemed simply brushing past me on the sidewalk would contaminate their femininity. One of them was my own sister, Katherine. When she shunned me, I can't say it didn't hurt. It's funny how hateful looks carry more weight than kind ones. I guess they feel more true.

I was careful with what I shot. There were men around who killed for pleasure. Game hogs, folks called them. Hunters who'd fire at anything that moved for the sheer joy of hitting a target. It didn't matter whether or not the creature was edible. That kind of slaughter sickened me. So I was selective. If a deer was nursing a fawn, I let her be. If quails were raising their chicks, I didn't bother them.

I had to give some of what I earned over to Ma for board and lodging, but I was saving every last cent I could. Then one day when I was delivering rabbits to the store Mr Wagner showed me a new gun.

I fell in love with it at first sight. The rifle was a sleek, gleaming thing and I couldn't help running my fingers over the brass inlay on the butt.

"I can't afford that," I told him.

"It's a gift," Mr Wagner said.

I blushed to the roots of my hair.

Before I had a chance to reply, he added, "No ... not a gift ... an investment. A business investment. You shoot more, I sell more and we both reap the profit. Deal?"

"Deal," I replied. I was terrible fond of Pa's rifle, but I was also practical. This new one was a breech loader. I could fire twice as often, twice as fast. I knew Ma would think that accepting a gift from a man I wasn't married to was akin to prostitution. But I curtsied and I blushed, and I took it.

23.

Now, I knew nothing about politics or history
or the government, but it was those things that
turned my life on its head.

Since Pa died, all I'd been doing was
surviving. I hadn't looked any further than the
end of my own nose. I'd been raised in one tiny
part of one little county in one small state on
the eastern side of the United States of America.
Indians had been cleared off the land long before
I was born.

But sometimes wild tales of what was
happening out west would stir up the grown-ups.
I remember Mrs Rogers shaking with shock when
General George Armstrong Custer was killed
at Little Bighorn. Mr Rogers had lined us all
up and told the whole sorry story with a catch
in his voice. He said a bunch of savages led by
the brutal chief Sitting Bull had slaughtered the

finest general in the US army along with every single one of his valiant men. With tears in his eyes he declared it had been an all-out massacre, the very worst Indian atrocity in the history of America. And those savages would surely pay for it.

The little ones had made a game of it afterwards, acting out the battle. The boys fought over who would be Sitting Bull and who would be Custer and get to die in the most tragical manner.

For me it was too distant a thing to concern myself with. I never gave Custer or Sitting Bull or the Indian wars out west a second thought. All I knew was that there were no more Indian victories after Little Bighorn. By the time I left the infirmary, the days of America's Wild West were over and done with. The Indians had been beaten once and for all. What was left of them had been moved on to government reservations and settlers were farming what had once been their land.

When a thing's happening, and it's fresh and wild and dangerous, grown folk are terrified of it. They suck their teeth, they shake their heads, they frown and blame the government and say something should be done. But when it's over, when it's all in the past, they develop a kind of fondness for it. They soften the edges of the horror and the cruelty and start telling stories, embellishing them – making them bigger, grander, more heroic.

The entire country had more or less reached that stage when I started supplying game to the Wagners' store. Folk in the eastern states were greedily gobbling up tales from the old Wild West. The thrilling excitement! The danger! The bravery! The courage of the pioneering souls who set out to build this great nation of America!

There were plenty of people prepared to make a few dollars out of that hunger. Showmen were touring the eastern states, putting on displays of rough riding and cattle roping and Indian fighting and lord alone knows what else.

On top of all that, there were marksmen, showing off their skill with a rifle.

And sometimes those very same marksmen challenged the local hicks to a shooting match.

24.

I would never, ever, not in a hundred thousand years, have put myself forward for a competition. But when Mr Wagner took me aside one morning and said he'd entered me in a shooting match, I didn't step away from it.

It seemed a stranger had come to town. Mr Wagner had been making a delivery to the hotel along the street when he'd heard a man boasting that he could beat any local shooter who cared to take him on.

"I told him I knew someone who'd beat him," Mr Wagner said. "You'll do it, won't you, Miss Maggie?"

I knew full well that Ma would die if I agreed to parade myself in public like that. But the way I saw it, I had no choice.

There was a prize.

One hundred dollars.

One.

Hundred.

Dollars.

I'd already saved one hundred dollars, but it had taken me more than a year. If I won another hundred in just one afternoon, I'd have enough money to buy the farm outright. Ma could stop worrying about the bank foreclosing on the mortgage. Mr Crawley could breathe easy. He'd know that if – *when* – he died, Ma and the children wouldn't be thrown out on the streets to starve.

Now wasn't that a prize worth sacrificing every last shred of respectability for?

25.

Mr Wagner had said I was a local shooter. He'd implied I was some barefoot hick from a cabin out in the woods. He never mentioned the fact that I was female.

The competition took place that very afternoon. Mr Wagner hadn't said my name, yet rumours started up and were soon being whispered from mouth to mouth. The air was buzzing with excitement. I prayed to God that there was no time for anyone to go galloping off to tell Ma what I was about to do. And if they did? I prayed to Pa she wouldn't get here before the whole thing was over.

There was a ring marked out with poles and ropes in a field at the edge of town. The shooter had a group of strangers with him. I figured they must do this kind of thing in every town they came to, because it was all awful well organised.

There were pigeons in cages that would be released one at a time. A man was yelling his head off, telling the gathered crowd that the two competitors would have twenty-five shots each. Whoever brought the most birds down would win the one-hundred-dollar prize.

The man announced my opponent, Mr Frank Wilkes, and he walked into the ring.

I'd had about an hour to get my head straight. I knew what I was facing. My opponent didn't. My name was called, but it was drowned out by a cheer from the crowd. When I walked into that ring, the cigar dropped from Mr Frank Wilkes's mouth and he darned nearly shot his own foot off by accident.

I'd unsettled him.

Good.

Trouble was, he'd unsettled me too.

Mrs Rogers might have told me I was old enough to be thinking about a home of my own, but the truth was that thoughts of men and marriage were about as far from my head as the moon. I didn't want any man touching me and I most certainly didn't want to be obeying one.

But the man standing there with a shotgun in his hand and a look of utter shock on his face was the most good-looking creature I'd ever seen. I don't mean handsome. Handsome men ain't worth a cent. They're so busy admiring themselves in the mirror that there ain't no point anyone else doing it. I mean good looking in the sense that he looked good. He looked honest. Kind. Trustworthy. And I found myself thinking, *What in the heck is a man like you doing in a place like this?* and *How long are you staying?*

The competition started. The crowd hushed down.

And then it was just me. And my gun. And the target.

Frank Wilkes was good.

But I was better.

It might have helped that every soul in town was with me. Even the women who crossed the street to avoid me were on my side against an outsider. I could feel them willing my bullets to hit the target. And every time I did, they cheered. I could hear Katherine's voice in among them and it lifted my heart.

By the time we'd finished, Mr Frank Wilkes had brought down twenty-three birds.

I'd shot twenty-four.

26.

When my last bird hit the ground, the crowd whooped and cheered and I stood there, beside a man who made his living as a professional sharpshooter. The showman Frank Wilkes had just been beaten by a slip of a girl, a nobody from a hick town in a hick county in a hick state. Any man alive could be forgiven for feeling his pride had been badly bruised.

I didn't want to look at Frank. But I couldn't stop my eyes sliding sideways.

He was smiling at me, shy-like. His mouth was open, but he seemed to be struggling with what to say. And of course, I had no idea how to break the silence.

But just then a big black dog came bounding over the field towards us, all hair and teeth and pink-tongued grin. The dog jumped right up at Frank, almost knocking him off his feet.

"Hey, Sam," he said, ruffling the dog's ears. "You been watching me? Ain't you mortified to see your master get beat so bad?" Frank fussed the dog a moment more, then told it to sit. He said, "Now look here, Sam. This lady here's the finest shot I ever did see. She beat me fair and square. I think you better make friends with her."

Sam looked up at me and raised a paw. I took it, gave it a shake. I said, "My name's Maggie McGregor. Very pleased to meet you, Sam."

Frank sighed and there seemed an awful lot of regret in it. "You'd better say your goodbyes, Sam," Frank said. "We have to be off on the next train."

"Oh," I said to the dog. I couldn't hide the disappointment in my voice, but I still couldn't look at Frank. "That's a pity. I was hoping to get better acquainted with you, Sam."

Frank turned to go and the feeling of loss that washed over me was overwhelming. But then he swung back, flushing scarlet, and said, "Can I write you?"

"No!" I said. The idea horrified me. If a letter arrived at the farm, Ma would know I'd picked up a man – a perfect stranger – whom no one knew anything about! But the prospect of never seeing Frank again was even worse. So I said, real quick, "*You* can't. But your dog might care to. Send it to the Wagners' store. I can pick up mail from there."

27.

Word about the competition reached Ma long
before I got home. I hung around behind the
barn, out of sight, biding my time to make my
entrance. Mr Crawley was sleeping and Ma was
feeding the chickens when I snuck in to the cabin
and arranged two hundred dollars carefully
on the table. One hundred dollar bills in prize
money spread out in a fan. Another hundred in
coins stacked in neat piles. It was the proudest
moment of my life. It sure looked pretty. With
all that money on display, Ma couldn't say a word
against me.

Could she?

"That'll pay off the mortgage, won't it?" I said
when she came back in and saw the table.

It wasn't a question. We both knew it would.

There was no point waiting for Ma to reply.
I'd struck her dumb.

"I figured you'd want to take it to the bank yourself," I told her. "Or I could do it, next time I'm in town."

The look on her face is hard to describe. A hundred thoughts seemed to travel across it all at once, tugging her muscles in different directions. And then it settled down and she mostly looked confused that she'd somehow been out-manoeuvred.

I stared at the floor, thinking Ma would probably still disapprove of me. She'd probably still dislike every single thing I did. She'd certainly still blame me for killing Pa, because if it hadn't been for me and my birthday he'd never have gone into town that day. But a bubble of hope was swelling under my ribs. Maybe this was the moment things would change between her and me? I felt a slight shift, as if the balance of God's Creation was tilting in my favour.

Ma owed me now. My actions had saved the family. I'd forced her to be grateful for my existence. Surely now she'd feel differently about me? That bubble of hope made me lift up my eyes, look Ma full in the face and smile.

She looked like she was itching to slap me.

28.

Mr Crawley was truly grateful. He told me I was the most loving, the most kind daughter anyone could ever hope to have. He thanked me with tears in his eyes and a hand on his heart and such a look of relief on his face that for a moment I feared I might have killed him. He'd been clinging to life for the sake of Ma and the children. Now they were safe, maybe he'd think he was free to die?

But he didn't. Not that night, anyway. He seemed to sleep a whole lot easier, but I didn't.

In all honesty, what I'd done for Mr Crawley and the family was less from loving kindness and more from a bull-headed desperate desire to prove I was worth something. I knew it. Ma knew it. So the atmosphere in the cabin wasn't improved by the fact that they now owned it outright.

If it hadn't been for Frank and the letter that arrived at the store the very next day, I think I'd have gone clean out of my mind.

Mr Wagner pushed the envelope across the counter, saying, "Looks like you got yourself an admirer."

I was so aflame with embarrassment I nearly burned to ashes right there in the store. I stuffed the letter in my pocket and walked deep into the woods where no one could see me read it.

It was written on hotel notepaper in a fine flowing hand.

Dear Miss Maggie,

(May I call you Maggie? Being a dog, I'm not entirely sure of human etiquette. I hope you don't think me impolite?)

Anyways, I have a problem which I'm hoping you might be able to solve.

Today my master was beaten by a girl who stands five foot nothing. He lost one hundred dollars in prize money. That girl was you, as I presume you recall, unless you make a habit of whupping men in shooting competitions? Maybe they're a dime a dozen?

Now I was expecting my master's pride to be wounded, because he don't like being beat, but something mighty strange has happened to him. When we got on the train, he was humming to himself and he had a great big smile slapped across his face. But as we pulled out of the station, he started to look real sad, and the further we went the sadder he looked and the more he sighed.

I figured he was sick, but then he started talking, and it was all about you, Miss Maggie.

"Did you see the way she smiled, Sam?" my master said. "Did you hear the softness of her voice? Have you ever seen anyone so dainty? So pretty? And oh my! Have you ever seen anyone fire a gun like that? She's got to be the finest shot I have ever seen!"

Well, I'd been right there and watched the whole shooting match, and I tried to tell my master that by yawning right in his face. But still he kept on going over and over everything you'd done and everything you'd said.

I figure he's caught you like a fever, Miss Maggie, and I don't rightly know what to do about it.

Could you maybe write me – care of the hotel where we'll be staying for the next five days? Please tell me if he's got any chance at all of winning your heart?

If I'm being too forward, please forgive me. Courtship among us canines is a much more straightforward matter. I ain't really sure how to deal with the situation between human beings.

If you don't send a letter, I will do my best to explain to my master that there is no hope of you returning his affection. But he will take a heap of comforting and I ain't sure I got enough licks in my tongue for that job.

Anxiously yours,
Sam.

And then there was an inky paw print.

Frank made me laugh. He made my heart beat nineteen to the dozen. And he gave a glimpse of a world that was bigger and brighter

than the one I'd lived in all my life. Of course
I fell in love with him. How could I possibly do
anything else?

29.

Word soon got to Ma that someone was sending me letters. She asked outright if I was corresponding with a man and I told her the truth: "No. I'm writing to a dog."

That didn't help matters much.

We wrote each other daily, Sam and I. To begin with, it was silly nonsense that made me smile. But the longer it went on – and it went on for months – the more serious it got. I told that dog things I'd never told another living soul. I told him how I felt when I was out alone in the woods, and how I could still hear the beat of fairy wings if I kept still for long enough. I told Sam how Pa had taken me with him when I was a child and I told him about my father dying and my mother leaving me at the infirmary. I told him how things stood between Ma and me. The writing of it all there in black and white lightened the weight of it somehow. But I never once mentioned the shark man and his shark wife. I just couldn't bring myself to set that down on paper.

And then one day Sam told me his master was in a dreadful state of indecision. He wanted to propose to me, but he wasn't sure he should.

Sam wrote:

My master is an honest man, Miss Maggie. He doesn't smoke, he doesn't drink and he doesn't gamble. He may be a showman – shooting his rifle is just about the only way he knows to make money – but he's known what it is to be poor and he's careful with what he earns. But there's one thing about him that some folk find scandalous. My master was married once. It was a big mistake and they got divorced not long after, but it still troubles some people real bad. Can you forgive my master, Miss Maggie? Should he propose to you? Write straight back if you can. If you can't ... he'll understand.

A proposal?

I felt a crushing weight pressing down on my shoulders. Loving Frank was one thing. But marrying a man meant sharing a bed with him. It meant doing things that made babies grow. And the idea of Frank touching me – the idea of him doing the kind of things the shark man had done – made me feel sick to the depths of my belly.

It took me a long time to reply to his letter. I kept starting, but my hand was shaking so much the pen wouldn't form the words I needed. I don't know how many sheets of paper I messed up. In the end, I prayed to Pa to help me. I took a very deep breath and finally I wrote back:

Sam, I ain't scandalised in the least. For what it's worth, I forgive your master. How could I do anything else? I know full well what a good man he is – I saw that the moment I laid eyes on him. Truly, I love him with all my heart. But there's something he needs to know. He's confessed to me, now I've got something I need to confess to him. It's difficult for me to write it. I don't even like to think it, but he can't go asking me to marry him unless he knows the truth. When I was a child, I was hired out as a maid to a couple for about a year. The man forced himself on me. I was hurt bad. So bad that I don't think I can be with a man the way a wife should be with a husband.

It was all I could bring myself to write on the subject. But if Frank was half as understanding as he seemed, he'd know what I was getting at. I mailed it off to him.

I thought that would be it. I'd lived in a golden glowing dream these last few months, but now it was over. I couldn't see me getting any kind of reply after my revelation. I was soiled goods. No man in his right mind would want me.

No more letters came to the Wagners' store.

But ten long days later I got up at dawn to go hunting the way I always did. When I opened the door, Sam was sitting on the step with a piece of paper in his mouth.

There were just two words written on it.

"Marry me?"

30.

Frank was waiting in the shadows on the far side of the yard when Sam gave me the note. I put it in my pocket with a smile on my face.

When I stepped down off the porch and walked across the yard, Frank fell into step beside me. Without a word, we slipped into the woods where we could talk without being disturbed.

I was so very, very happy to see him! But somehow I couldn't say so. We'd been talking freely on paper. But things were a whole lot more awkward face to face – without Sam as a go-between. I wanted to melt into Frank's arms the way women did in fairy tales. I wanted him to carry me away on the saddle of his horse like a knight in shining armour. I wanted him to be poetic and passionate. Yet when he looked as if he might be about to embrace me, I froze.

Frank stepped back, raised his hands and said, "I ain't going to touch you. I won't ever touch you, not unless you ask me to." He wiped his palms on his trousers. He was sweating, stuttering, stumbling over his words.

"Look, I got things to say," Frank said. "There's an idea that's been banging away in my head since the time we first met. I'm just going to say it all, get it off my chest. If you don't like it, why, then I can walk away and you don't ever have to see me again. I want to marry you, Maggie, I already told you that. I loved you from the moment you stepped out into that shooting ring. And I know that maybe I can't ever touch you, but that don't matter to me. I want your company. Your friendship. That would be enough. Hell, that's more than most married folks ever get! But the kind of work I do is hard. I spend all my time on the move. I sleep on trains or in cheap hotels. There ain't no glamour to being a showman and there's precious little money by the time I've paid for travel and food and all. With two of us on the road, things would be harder than ever. But there's a way I can see of making enough money for the both of us. I don't know if it's right me asking you, but if I don't I'll be kicking myself for the rest of my life …

"I want you up on stage with me. A double act. I know it ain't decent for a woman to be performing. If you come with me, you'd be mixing with actresses and gamblers and whores and God alone knows who else. I'll be dragging you away from home and I know how much the woods mean to you. I'll understand if you turn me down flat."

My mouth had dropped so far open my chin was scraping the forest floor.

A double act?

Me up on stage?

In front of strangers?

I would have been less surprised if Frank had said he could ride a bluebird and fly me to the moon.

All I managed to say was, "A double act?"

Frank looked relieved. At least I hadn't screamed in his face or swooned.

"Yeah," he said. "I figure we can work up an act so we can tour theatres, music halls and the like. The two of us would be a sensation if we get it right."

The prospect of leaving home and heading out into the unknown was dizzying. Terrifying.

Yet the idea of not doing it was even worse. I had a vision of me living in Ma's cabin for the rest of my life, dying an old maid, alone and forgotten. I shivered.

"I'll do it," I said. "Marry you. Work with you. I'm throwing my hat in the ring with yours."

The whoop Frank let rip from his chest sent birds flapping and screeching from the trees. Heck, it was almost loud enough to wake the dead!

31.

The second time I met Frank Wilkes in person was the very same day I married him.

Things moved fast because Frank had shows to do out west and there didn't seem any point in waiting. So we went to the preacher. Ma complained about the scandalous speed – everyone would think I had a baby on the way, she said – but she didn't make any kind of move to stop us.

Ma came to see us off at the train station in the evening. Mr Crawley kissed me fondly and wished me well. And Ma? I was truly off her hands at last. It was the first time I'd ever seen her smile.

I'd been such a fool to go back to Ma over and over again. Each time, I'd hoped to put things right, hoped that things would be different. I'd kept picking away at it like a scab, but the rift between Ma and me hadn't healed. How could it? All I'd done was give myself more pain. All I'd done was draw fresh blood.

Things were as they were. It was time to put it behind me. Time to walk away. The past was gone. But there was a future ahead of me.

I reached out, and I took Frank's hand in mine. His palm felt warm. It felt safe.

It felt like home.

Together, we boarded the train.

Author's note

One Shot is a work of fiction inspired by the real-life "rags to riches" story of Annie Oakley – America's first female celebrity.

Annie Oakley was the highest paid performer in Buffalo Bill's Wild West show. At a time when women didn't have the vote and their career options were largely limited to marriage and motherhood, it was an extraordinary achievement.

The "slip of a girl" from Ohio first picked up a gun when she was eight years old, hunting to put food on her family's table. By the age of twenty-two, Annie was performing for money and could outshoot any competitor. She travelled the world, performing to audiences that included Queen Victoria, and displayed her marksmanship by snuffing out candles and knocking corks from bottles.

Wherever she went, Annie captured people's hearts. Sitting Bull, chief of the Lakota Sioux, toured with the Wild West show in 1885. He and Annie became such close friends that they spoke of each other as adopted father and daughter. She became an international superstar, with acres of newsprint devoted to her. Yet behind her public face, little of her background was revealed.

I used events from Annie's childhood as a trigger for the story, but *One Shot* isn't her biography. It's an imagined tale of how it might have felt to have had a childhood like hers and to emerge from those dark days into the dazzling bright lights of global stardom.

Our books are tested
for children and young people by
children and young people.

Thanks to everyone who consulted on
a manuscript for their time and effort in
helping us to make our books better
for our readers.